Library of Congress Cataloging-in-Publication Data

Philip, Neil.
    Prince Zucchini / retold by Neil Philip ; after a story by Jeanne
-Marie Leprince de Beaumont ; art by Veronica Rooney.
        p. cm.
    Summary: As a result of a sorcerer's curse, Prince Zucchini is
born with a very large nose, but he does not realize it until he
falls in love with a small-nosed princess.
    ISBN 1-887734-98-8
    [1. Fairy tales. 2. Nose--Fiction. 3. Self-perception--Fiction.]
I. Leprince de Beaumont, Madame (Jeanne-Marie), 1711-1780.
II. Rooney, Veronica, ill. III. Title.
PZ8.P54Pr 2002
398.2 E--dc21

2002012758

Prince Zucchini

Retold by
NEIL PHILIP

After a story by
JEANNE-MARIE LEPRINCE DE BEAUMONT

Art by
VERONICA ROONEY

Star Bright Books
New York

Once upon a time there was a king who was very vain. He was never bored because when he had nothing to do, he would sit and twiddle the ends of his mustache, thinking, "How handsome I am!"

One day the king saw a beautiful princess with a glossy, black cat following her. He spoke to her, but she didn't hear him; she only had eyes for her cat. And so the king fell in love with the one princess who never gave him a second glance, and he decided to win her heart.

The cat followed the princess, and the king followed both of them. He kept hoping the princess would notice him, but she never did. That made the king so sad that the twirly ends of his mustache began to droop. He just couldn't understand why she was not interested in him.

Stepping back from a mirror one day, the king stepped on the cat's tail. The creature leaped up with a terrible screech, and as it did so, it turned into a tall sorcerer. The princess was so frightened that she jumped straight into the king's arms. Her beloved cat wasn't a cat at all!

The sorcerer growled at the king, "You have broken my spell and won the princess away from me. But I will have my revenge. Your first son will have a nose like the biggest zucchini you ever saw. Everyone will laugh at him. And when he realizes how stupid he looks, he will be unhappy. And there's nothing you can do about it."

"That's not fair!" cried the king. But the sorcerer had already disappeared.

The king and the princess were married, and before long the queen gave birth to a baby boy. He was perfect. Ten little fingers and ten little toes. Two blue eyes, pink round cheeks, a rosebud mouth—and the longest, fattest, silliest nose in the whole world! The king took one look at him and fainted from the shock.

The queen took one look at him and said, "Oh! Diddums darling! Aren't you the sweetest little baby that ever there was?" And then she said, "I shall call him Zucchero," which means sugar. But when the prince was christened, though the priest knew full well he was to be called Prince Zucchero, the wrong words came out his mouth.

"I christen you Prince Zucchini," he said before he could stop himself. So that was what the prince was called.

Prince Zucchini grew up a happy lad. His mother never thought there was anything strange about him. But his father scoured the land for people with big noses to be his son's servants, so the boy would not feel at all odd. Every night he was lulled to sleep with fairy tales about brave heroes with enormous honkers.

No one laughed at the prince's nose. Everyone pulled their own noses every day to try to make them bigger. Some of the servants even wore false noses over their own normal-size noses. So instead of feeling unhappy, the prince grew up sweet-tempered and cheerful.

When Prince Zucchini was ready to find a wife, the king of a neighboring land sent a portrait of his daughter. Everyone in the castle laughed at it. "Look at that poor, unfortunate girl!" they said. "She must be embarrassed by her funny snub-nose. Do you suppose they call her Pug Face?"

The princess did have a little nose that tilted up at the end, but Prince Zucchini was a kind-hearted young man, and he didn't like them mocking her. "I think she looks lovely," he said. "I don't care what you all say," he declared, "I think she looks like a dear little princess." And that, funnily enough, was her name, Dear Little Princess. So after that, the servants started saying, "Well, of course, a nose isn't everything," and "Perhaps it will grow." And Prince Zucchini said, "I love her just as she is, small nose or not."

So he set off on his horse for the neighboring kingdom to ask for the Dear Little Princess's hand in marriage. The prince was so eager to leave that he didn't bother to look in his saddlebag. If he had, he would have seen that a glossy black cat was hitching a ride!

It was the sorcerer, who was furious that his curse hadn't worked. He had wanted the prince to be unhappy, but instead he was one of the happiest princes who had ever lived! The sight of Prince Zucchini, riding along without a care in the world and singing silly love songs at the top of his voice, made the enchanted cat want to spit!

The evil cat waited until Prince Zucchini arrived at the court and went down on one knee to kiss the hand of the Dear Little Princess. Then the cat sprang from the saddlebag, turned into the sorcerer, and with a horrible laugh snatched the Dear Little Princess away. "You'll never find her till you learn to see yourself as others see you!" he shouted. And at that, the sorcerer and the Dear Little Princess vanished.

The prince rode far and wide in search of the Dear Little Princess. He thought it was very unfair that his true love should have been whisked away so suddenly. At last he came to a palace deep in the forest and went inside to ask whether anyone had seen the Dear Little Princess. There was nobody about, and nothing much there, except for a throne with a red velvet cushion and a bowl of milk on the floor. Prince Zucchini didn't know it, but he was in the evil sorcerer's palace.

Prince Zucchini shouted, "Is anybody here?" but there was no reply—just the sound of his own voice echoing through the empty halls. Prince Zucchini went from room to room in the palace, looking for the Dear Little Princess. He saw a strange light shining beneath the door to the last room. When he opened the door, he discovered that he was standing in a huge hall of mirrors.

There were mirrors on every wall, and Prince Zucchini saw the Dear Little Princess reflected in every one. The sorcerer had trapped her inside the glass! But which reflection was the real princess? Prince Zucchini went to each in turn. They all looked the same, except that one of the mirrors had a flaw in the glass. When the prince looked closer, he saw that it wasn't a flaw at all, but a real teardrop on the Dear Little Princess's cheek.

When she saw how sad he looked, and how determined he was to free her, the Dear Little Princess's heart melted. The prince had ridden halfway across the world to rescue her. She looked at Prince Zucchini and didn't notice his nose at all. She saw only his bright kind eyes and his kind face. She loved him at first sight. Without thinking, she puckered up her lips for a kiss.

Now Prince Zucchini had heard plenty
of fairy tales in which the princess was
freed from enchantment by a kiss.

In the ones he had been told, the awakened beauty was always particularly impressed by the prince's fine nose. So he puckered up his lips and tried to place them against the glass. But he couldn't! His nose was in the way.

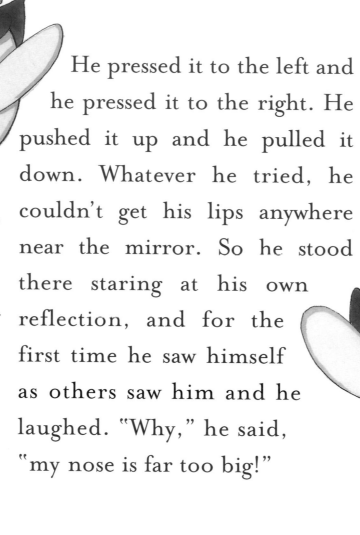

He pressed it to the left and he pressed it to the right. He pushed it up and he pulled it down. Whatever he tried, he couldn't get his lips anywhere near the mirror. So he stood there staring at his own reflection, and for the first time he saw himself as others saw him and he laughed. "Why," he said, "my nose is far too big!"

Then everything happened at once. The sorcerer's curse was finally broken, and Prince Zucchini's enormous nose shrank to half its size (which still wasn't small, but it was an improvement). The mirror fell to pieces at the Dear Little Princess' feet, and Prince Zucchini's lips met those of the Dear Little Princess in a delicious kiss.

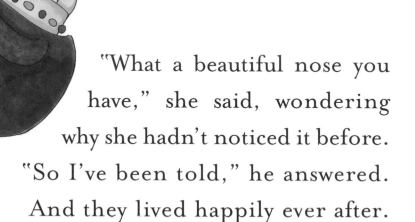

"What a beautiful nose you have," she said, wondering why she hadn't noticed it before. "So I've been told," he answered. And they lived happily ever after.

As for the evil cat, he was chased up a tree by the prince's dog and never came down again.